I0766927

†

Solomon Kane: Vol I

Robert E. Howard

HAMMER

TABLE OF CONTENTS

RED SHADOWS

SKULLS IN THE STARS

RATTLE OF BONES

†

R ED S HADOWS

I

T HE C OMING OF S OLOMON

The moonlight shimmered hazily, making silvery mists of illusion among the shadowy trees. A faint breeze whispered down the valley, bearing a shadow that was not of the moon-mist. A faint scent of smoke was apparent.

The man whose long, swinging strides, unhurried yet unswerving, had carried him for many a mile since sunrise, stopped suddenly. A movement in the trees had caught his attention, and he moved silently toward the shadows, a hand resting lightly on the hilt of his long, slim rapier.

Warily he advanced, his eyes striving to pierce the darkness that brooded under the trees. This was a wild and menacing country; death might be lurking under those trees. Then his hand fell away from the hilt and he leaned forward. Death indeed was there, but not in such shape as might cause him fear.

†

"The fires of Hades!" he murmured. "A girl! What has harmed you, child? Be not afraid of me."

The girl looked up at him, her face like a dim white rose in the dark.

"You—who are—you?" her words came in gasps.

"Naught but a wanderer, a landless man, but a friend to all in need." The gentle voice sounded somehow incongruous, coming from the man.

The girl sought to prop herself up on her elbow, and instantly he knelt and raised her to a sitting position, her head resting against his shoulder. His hand touched her breast and came away red and wet.

"Tell me." His voice was soft, soothing, as one speaks to a babe.

"Le Loup," she gasped, her voice swiftly growing weaker. "He and his men—descended upon our village—a mile up the valley. They robbed—slew—burned—"

"That, then, was the smoke I scented," muttered the man. "Go on, child."

"I ran. He, the Wolf, pursued me—and—caught me—" The words died away in a shuddering silence.

"I understand, child. Then—?"

†

"Then—he—he—stabbed me—with his dagger—oh, blessed saints!—mercy—"

Suddenly the slim form went limp. The man eased her to the earth, and touched her brow lightly.

"Dead!" he muttered.

Slowly he rose, mechanically wiping his hands upon his cloak. A dark scowl had settled on his somber brow. Yet he made no wild, reckless vow, swore no oath by saints or devils.

"Men shall die for this," he said coldly.

†

II

The Lair of the Wolf

"**Y**ou are a fool!" The words came in a cold snarl that curdled the hearer's blood.

He who had just been named a fool lowered his eyes sullenly without answer.

"You and all the others I lead!" The speaker leaned forward, his fist pounding emphasis on the rude table between them. He was a tall, rangy-built man, supple as a leopard and with a lean, cruel, predatory face. His eyes danced and glittered with a kind of reckless mockery.

The fellow spoken to replied sullenly, "This Solomon Kane is a demon from hell, I tell you."

"Faugh! Dolt! He is a man—who will die from a pistol ball or a sword thrust."

"So thought Jean, Juan and La Costa," answered the other grimly. "Where are they? Ask the mountain wolves that tore the flesh from their dead bones. Where does this Kane hide? We have searched the mountains and the valleys for leagues, and we have found no trace.

†

I tell you, Le Loup, he comes up from hell. I knew no good would come from hanging that friar a moon ago."

The Wolf strummed impatiently upon the table. His keen face, despite lines of wild living and dissipation, was the face of a thinker. The superstitions of his followers affected him not at all.

"Faugh! I say again. The fellow has found some cavern or secret vale of which we do not know where he hides in the day."

"And at night he sallies forth and slays us," gloomily commented the other. "He hunts us down as a wolf hunts deer—by God, Le Loup, you name yourself Wolf but I think you have met at last a fiercer and more crafty wolf than yourself! The first we know of this man is when we find Jean, the most desperate bandit unhung, nailed to a tree with his own dagger through his breast, and the letters *S. L. K.* carved upon his dead cheeks. Then the Spaniard Juan is struck down, and after we find him he lives long enough to tell us that the slayer is an Englishman, Solomon Kane, who has sworn to destroy our entire band! What then? La Costa, a swordsman second only to yourself, goes forth swearing to meet this Kane. By the demons of perdition, it seems he met him! For we found his sword-pierced corpse upon a cliff. What now? Are we all to fall before this English fiend?"

✝

"True, our best men have been done to death by him," mused the bandit chief. "Soon the rest return from that little trip to the hermit's; then we shall see. Kane can not hide forever. Then—ha, what was that?"

The two turned swiftly as a shadow fell across the table. Into the entrance of the cave that formed the bandit lair, a man staggered. His eyes were wide and staring; he reeled on buckling legs, and a dark red stain dyed his tunic. He came a few tottering steps forward, then pitched across the table, sliding off onto the floor.

"Hell's devils!" cursed the Wolf, hauling him upright and propping him in a chair. "Where are the rest, curse you?"

"Dead! All dead!"

"How? Satan's curses on you, speak!" The Wolf shook the man savagely, the other bandit gazing on in wide-eyed horror.

"We reached the hermit's hut just as the moon rose," the man muttered. "I stayed outside—to watch—the others went in—to torture the hermit—to make him reveal—the hiding-place—of his gold."

"Yes, yes! Then what?" The Wolf was raging with impatience.

"Then the world turned red—the hut went up in a roar and a red rain flooded the valley—through it I saw—the hermit and a tall man clad all in black—coming from the trees—"

9

✝

"Solomon Kane!" gasped the bandit. "I knew it! I—"

"Silence, fool!" snarled the chief. "Go on!"

"I fled—Kane pursued—wounded me—but I outran—him—got—here—first—"

The man slumped forward on the table.

"Saints and devils!" raged the Wolf. "What does he look like, this Kane?"

"Like—Satan—"

The voice trailed off in silence. The dead man slid from the table to lie in a red heap upon the floor.

"Like Satan!" babbled the other bandit. "I told you! 'Tis the Horned One himself! I tell you—"

He ceased as a frightened face peered in at the cave entrance.

"Kane?"

"Aye." The Wolf was too much at sea to lie. "Keep close watch, La Mon; in a moment the Rat and I will join you."

The face withdrew and Le Loup turned to the other.

"This ends the band," said he. "You, I, and that thief La Mon are all that are left. What would you suggest?"

The Rat's pallid lips barely formed the word: "Flight!"

✝

"You are right. Let us take the gems and gold from the chests and flee, using the secret passageway."

"And La Mon?"

"He can watch until we are ready to flee. Then—why divide the treasure three ways?"

A faint smile touched the Rat's malevolent features. Then a sudden thought smote him.

"He," indicating the corpse on the floor, "said, 'I got here first.' Does that mean Kane was pursuing him here?" And as the Wolf nodded impatiently the other turned to the chests with chattering haste.

The flickering candle on the rough table lighted up a strange and wild scene. The light, uncertain and dancing, gleamed redly in the slowly widening lake of blood in which the dead man lay; it danced upon the heaps of gems and coins emptied hastily upon the floor from the brassbound chests that ranged the walls; and it glittered in the eyes of the Wolf with the same gleam which sparkled from his sheathed dagger.

The chests were empty, their treasure lying in a shimmering mass upon the bloodstained floor. The Wolf stopped and listened. Outside was silence. There was no moon, and Le Loup's keen imagination pictured the dark slayer, Solomon Kane, gliding through the blackness, a shadow

†

among shadows. He grinned crookedly; this time the Englishman would be foiled.

"There is a chest yet unopened," said he, pointing.

The Rat, with a muttered exclamation of surprise, bent over the chest indicated. With a single, catlike motion, the Wolf sprang upon him, sheathing his dagger to the hilt in the Rat's back, between the shoulders. The Rat sagged to the floor without a sound.

"Why divide the treasure two ways?" murmured Le Loup, wiping his blade upon the dead man's doublet. "Now for La Mon."

He stepped toward the door; then stopped and shrank back.

At first he thought that it was the shadow of a man who stood in the entrance; then he saw that it was a man himself, though so dark and still he stood that a fantastic semblance of shadow was lent him by the guttering candle.

A tall man, as tall as Le Loup he was, clad in black from head to foot, in plain, close-fitting garments that somehow suited the somber face. Long arms and broad shoulders betokened the swordsman, as plainly as the long rapier in his hand. The features of the man were saturnine and gloomy. A kind of dark pallor lent him a ghostly appearance in the uncertain light, an effect heightened by the satanic darkness of his

✝

lowering brows. Eyes, large, deep-set and unblinking, fixed their gaze upon the bandit, and looking into them, Le Loup was unable to decide what color they were. Strangely, the mephistophelean trend of the lower features was offset by a high, broad forehead, though this was partly hidden by a featherless hat.

That forehead marked the dreamer, the idealist, the introvert, just as the eyes and the thin, straight nose betrayed the fanatic. An observer would have been struck by the eyes of the two men who stood there, facing each other. Eyes of both betokened untold deeps of power, but there the resemblance ceased.

The eyes of the bandit were hard, almost opaque, with a curious scintillant shallowness that reflected a thousand changing lights and gleams, like some strange gem; there was mockery in those eyes, cruelty and recklessness.

The eyes of the man in black, on the other hand, deep-set and staring from under prominent brows, were cold but deep; gazing into them, one had the impression of looking into countless fathoms of ice.

Now the eyes clashed, and the Wolf, who was used to being feared, felt a strange coolness on his spine. The sensation was new to him—a new thrill to one who lived for thrills, and he laughed suddenly.

†

"You are Solomon Kane, I suppose?" he asked, managing to make his question sound politely incurious.

"I am Solomon Kane." The voice was resonant and powerful. "Are you prepared to meet your God?"

"Why, Monsieur," Le Loup answered, bowing, "I assure you I am as ready as I ever will be. I might ask Monsieur the same question."

"No doubt I stated my inquiry wrongly," Kane said grimly. "I will change it: Are you prepared to meet your master, the Devil?"

"As to that, Monsieur"—Le Loup examined his finger nails with elaborate unconcern—"I must say that I can at present render a most satisfactory account to his Horned Excellency, though really I have no intention of so doing—for a while at least."

Le Loup did not wonder as to the fate of La Mon; Kane's presence in the cave was sufficient answer that did not need the trace of blood on his rapier to verify it.

"What I wish to know, Monsieur," said the bandit, "is why in the Devil's name have you harassed my band as you have, and how did you destroy that last set of fools?"

"Your last question is easily answered, sir," Kane replied. "I myself had the tale spread that the hermit possessed a store of gold, knowing that would draw your scum as carrion draws vultures. For days and nights I have watched the hut, and tonight, when I saw your villains coming, I warned the hermit, and together we went among the trees back of the hut. Then, when the rogues were inside, I struck flint and steel to the train I had laid, and flame ran through the trees like a red snake until it reached the powder I had placed beneath the hut floor. Then the hut and thirteen sinners went to hell in a great roar of flame and smoke. True, one escaped, but him I had slain in the forest had not I stumbled and fallen upon a broken root, which gave him time to elude me."

"Monsieur," said Le Loup with another low bow, "I grant you the admiration I must needs bestow on a brave and shrewd foeman. Yet tell me this: Why have you followed me as a wolf follows deer?"

"Some moons ago," said Kane, his frown becoming more menacing, "you and your fiends raided a small village down the valley. You know the details better than I. There was a girl there, a mere child, who, hoping to escape your lust, fled up the valley; but you, you jackal of hell, you caught her and left her, violated and dying. I found her there, and above her dead form I made up my mind to hunt you down and kill you."

"H'm," mused the Wolf. "Yes, I remember the wench. *Mon Dieu*, so the softer sentiments enter into the affair! Monsieur, I had not thought you an amorous man; be not jealous, good fellow, there are many more wenches."

†

"Le Loup, take care!" Kane exclaimed, a terrible menace in his voice, "I have never yet done a man to death by torture, but by God, sir, you tempt me!"

The tone, and more especially the unexpected oath, coming as it did from Kane, slightly sobered Le Loup; his eyes narrowed and his hand moved toward his rapier. The air was tense for an instant; then the Wolf relaxed elaborately.

"Who was the girl?" he asked idly, "Your wife?"

"I never saw her before," answered Kane.

"*Nom d'un nom!*" swore the bandit. "What sort of a man are you, Monsieur, who takes up a feud of this sort merely to avenge a wench unknown to you?"

"That, sir, is my own affair; it is sufficient that I do so."

Kane could not have explained, even to himself, nor did he ever seek an explanation within himself. A true fanatic, his promptings were reasons enough for his actions.

"You are right, Monsieur." Le Loup was sparring now for time; casually he edged backward inch by inch, with such consummate acting skill that he aroused no suspicion even in the hawk who watched him.

"Monsieur," said he, "possibly you will say that you are merely a noble cavalier, wandering about like a true Galahad, protecting the weaker;

but you and I know different. There on the floor is the equivalent to an emperor's ransom. Let us divide it peaceably; then if you like not my company, why—*nom d'un nom!*—we can go our separate ways."

Kane leaned forward, a terrible brooding threat growing in his cold eyes. He seemed like a great condor about to launch himself upon his victim.

"Sir, do you assume me to be as great a villain as yourself?"

Suddenly Le Loup threw back his head, his eyes dancing and leaping with a wild mockery and a kind of insane recklessness. His shout of laughter sent the echoes flying.

"Gods of hell! No, you fool, I do not class you with myself! *Mon Dieu,* Monsieur Kane, you have a task indeed if you intend to avenge all the wenches who have known my favors!"

"Shades of death! Shall I waste time in parleying with this base scoundrel!" Kane snarled in a voice suddenly blood-thirsting, and his lean frame flashed forward like a bent bow suddenly released.

At the same instant Le Loup with a wild laugh bounded backward with a movement as swift as Kane's. His timing was perfect; his back-flung hands struck the table and hurled it aside, plunging the cave into darkness as the candle toppled and went out.

Kane's rapier sang like an arrow in the dark as he thrust blindly and ferociously.

†

"*Adieu,* Monsieur Galahad!" The taunt came from somewhere in front of him, but Kane, plunging toward the sound with the savage fury of baffled wrath, caromed against a blank wall that did not yield to his blow. From somewhere seemed to come an echo of a mocking laugh.

Kane whirled, eyes fixed on the dimly outlined entrance, thinking his foe would try to slip past him and out of the cave; but no form bulked there, and when his groping hands found the candle and lighted it, the cave was empty, save for himself and the dead men on the floor.

†

III

THE CHANT OF THE DRUMS

Across the dusky waters the whisper came: *boom, boom, boom!*—a sullen reiteration. Far away and more faintly sounded a whisper of different timbre: *thrum, throom, thrum!* Back and forth went the vibrations as the throbbing drums spoke to each other. What tales did they carry? What monstrous secrets whispered across the sullen, shadowy reaches of the unmapped jungle?

"This, you are sure, is the bay where the Spanish ship put in?"

"Yes, *Senhor*, the negro swears this is the bay where the white man left the ship alone and went into the jungle."

Kane nodded grimly.

"Then put me ashore here, alone. Wait seven days; then if I have not returned and if you have no word of me, set sail wherever you will."

"Yes, *Senhor.*"

The waves slapped lazily against the sides of the boat that carried Kane ashore. The village that he sought was on the river bank but set back from the bay shore, the jungle hiding it from sight of the ship.

†

Kane had adopted what seemed the most hazardous course, that of going ashore by night, for the reason that he knew, if the man he sought were in the village, he would never reach it by day. As it was, he was taking a most desperate chance in daring the nighttime jungle, but all his life he had been used to taking desperate chances. Now he gambled his life upon the slim chance of gaining the negro village under cover of darkness and unknown to the villagers.

At the beach he left the boat with a few muttered commands, and as the rowers put back to the ship which lay anchored some distance out in the bay, he turned and engulfed himself in the blackness of the jungle. Sword in one hand, dagger in the other, he stole forward, seeking to keep pointed in the direction from which the drums still muttered and grumbled.

He went with the stealth and easy movement of a leopard, feeling his way cautiously, every nerve alert and straining, but the way was not easy. Vines tripped him and slapped him in the face, impeding his progress; he was forced to grope his way between the huge boles of towering trees, and all through the underbrush about him sounded vague and menacing rustlings and shadows of movement. Thrice his foot touched something that moved beneath it and writhed away, and once he glimpsed the baleful glimmer of feline eyes among the trees. They vanished, however, as he advanced.

$$\dagger$$

Thrum, thrum, thrum, came the ceaseless monotone of the drums: war and death (they said); blood and lust; human sacrifice and human feast! The soul of Africa (said the drums); the spirit of the jungle; the chant of the gods of outer darkness, the gods that roar and gibber, the gods men knew when dawns were young, beast-eyed, gaping-mouthed, huge-bellied, bloody-handed, the Black Gods (sang the drums).

All this and more the drums roared and bellowed to Kane as he worked his way through the forest. Somewhere in his soul a responsive chord was smitten and answered. You too are of the night (sang the drums); there is the strength of darkness, the strength of the primitive in you; come back down the ages; let us teach you, let us teach you (chanted the drums).

Kane stepped out of the thick jungle and came upon a plainly defined trail. Beyond, through the trees came the gleam of the village fires, flames glowing through the palisades. Kane walked down the trail swiftly.

He went silently and warily, sword extended in front of him, eyes straining to catch any hint of movement in the darkness ahead, for the trees loomed like sullen giants on each hand; sometimes their great branches intertwined above the trail and he could see only a slight way ahead of him.

Like a dark ghost he moved along the shadowed trail; alertly he stared

and harkened; yet no warning came first to him, as a great, vague bulk

rose up out of the shadows and struck him down, silently.

†

IV

THE BLACK GOD

Thrum, thrum, thrum! Somewhere, with deadening monotony, a cadence was repeated, over and over, bearing out the same theme: "Fool—fool—fool!" Now it was far away, now he could stretch out his hand and almost reach it. Now it merged with the throbbing in his head until the two vibrations were as one: "Fool—fool—fool—fool—"

The fogs faded and vanished. Kane sought to raise his hand to his head, but found that he was bound hand and foot. He lay on the floor of a hut—alone? He twisted about to view the place. No, two eyes glimmered at him from the darkness. Now a form took shape, and Kane, still mazed, believed that he looked on the man who had struck him unconscious. Yet no; this man could never strike such a blow. He was lean, withered and wrinkled. The only thing that seemed alive about him were his eyes, and they seemed like the eyes of a snake.

The man squatted on the floor of the hut, near the doorway, naked save for a loincloth and the usual paraphernalia of bracelets, anklets and armlets. Weird fetishes of ivory, bone and hide, animal and human, adorned his arms and legs. Suddenly and unexpectedly he spoke in English.

†

"Ha, you wake, white man? Why you come here, eh?"

Kane asked the inevitable question, following the habit of the Caucasian.

"You speak my language—how is that?"

The black man grinned.

"I slave—long time, me boy. Me, N'Longa, juju man, me, great fetish. No black man like me! You white man, you hunt brother?"

Kane snarled. "I! Brother! I seek a man, yes."

The negro nodded. "Maybe so you find um, eh?"

"He dies!"

Again the negro grinned. "Me pow'rful juju man," he announced apropos of nothing. He bent closer. "White man you hunt, eyes like a leopard, eh? Yes? *Ha! ha! ha! ha!* Listen, white man: man-with-eyes-of-a-leopard, he and Chief Songa make pow'rful palaver; they blood brothers now. Say nothing, I help you; you help me, eh?"

"Why should you help me?" asked Kane suspiciously.

The juju man bent closer and whispered, "White man Songa's right-hand man; Songa more pow'rful than N'Longa. White man mighty juju! N'Longa's white brother kill man-with-eyes-of-a-leopard, be blood

✝

brother to N'Longa, N'Longa be more pow'rful than Songa; palaver set."

And like a dusky ghost he floated out of the hut so swiftly that Kane was not sure but that the whole affair was a dream.

Without, Kane could see the flare of fires. The drums were still booming, but close at hand the tones merged and mingled, and the impulse-producing vibrations were lost. All seemed a barbaric clamor without rime or reason, yet there was an undertone of mockery there, savage and gloating. "Lies," thought Kane, his mind still swimming, "jungle lies like jungle women that lure a man to his doom."

Two warriors entered the hut—black giants, hideous with paint and armed with crude spears. They lifted the white man and carried him out of the hut. They bore him across an open space, leaned him upright against a post and bound him there. About him, behind him and to the side, a great semicircle of black faces leered and faded in the firelight as the flames leaped and sank. There in front of him loomed a shape hideous and obscene—a black, formless thing, a grotesque parody of the human. Still, brooding, bloodstained, like the formless soul of Africa, the horror, the Black God.

And in front and to each side, upon roughly carven thrones of teakwood, sat two men. He who sat upon the right was a black man, huge, ungainly, a gigantic and unlovely mass of dusky flesh and muscles.

†

Small, hog-like eyes blinked out over sin-marked cheeks; huge, flabby red lips pursed in fleshly haughtiness.

The other—

"Ah, Monsieur, we meet again." The speaker was far from being the debonair villain who had taunted Kane in the cavern among the mountains. His clothes were rags; there were more lines in his face; he had sunk lower in the years that had passed. Yet his eyes still gleamed and danced with their old recklessness and his voice held the same mocking timbre.

"The last time I heard that accursed voice," said Kane calmly, "was in a cave, in darkness, whence you fled like a hunted rat."

"Aye, under different conditions," answered Le Loup imperturbably. "What did you do after blundering about like an elephant in the dark?"

Kane hesitated, then: "I left the mountain—"

"By the front entrance? Yes? I might have known you were too stupid to find the secret door. Hoofs of the Devil, had you thrust against the chest with the golden lock, which stood against the wall, the door had opened to you and revealed the secret passageway through which I went."

"I traced you to the nearest port and there took ship and followed you to Italy, where I found you had gone."

†

"Aye, by the saints, you nearly cornered me in Florence. *Ho! ho! ho!* I was climbing through a back window while Monsieur Galahad was battering down the front door of the tavern. And had your horse not gone lame, you would have caught up with me on the road to Rome. Again, the ship on which I left Spain had barely put out to sea when Monsieur Galahad rides up to the wharfs. Why have you followed me like this? I do not understand."

"Because you are a rogue whom it is my destiny to kill," answered Kane coldly. He did not understand. All his life he had roamed about the world aiding the weak and fighting oppression, he neither knew nor questioned why. That was his obsession, his driving force of life. Cruelty and tyranny to the weak sent a red blaze of fury, fierce and lasting, through his soul. When the full flame of his hatred was wakened and loosed, there was no rest for him until his vengeance had been fulfilled to the uttermost. If he thought of it at all, he considered himself a fulfiller of God's judgment, a vessel of wrath to be emptied upon the souls of the unrighteous. Yet in the full sense of the word Solomon Kane was not wholly a Puritan, though he thought of himself as such.

Le Loup shrugged his shoulders. "I could understand had I wronged you personally. *Mon Dieu!* I, too, would follow an enemy across the world, but, though I would have joyfully slain and robbed you, I never heard of you until you declared war on me."

†

Kane was silent, his still fury overcoming him. Though he did not realize it, the Wolf was more than merely an enemy to him; the bandit symbolized, to Kane, all the things against which the Puritan had fought all his life: cruelty, outrage, oppression and tyranny.

Le Loup broke in on his vengeful meditations. "What did you do with the treasure, which—gods of Hades!—took me years to accumulate? Devil take it, I had time only to snatch a handful of coins and trinkets as I ran."

"I took such as I needed to hunt you down. The rest I gave to the villages which you had looted."

"Saints and the devil!" swore Le Loup. "Monsieur, you are the greatest fool I have yet met. To throw that vast treasure—by Satan, I rage to think of it in the hands of base peasants, vile villagers! Yet, ho! ho! ho! ho! they will steal, and kill each other for it! That is human nature."

"Yes, damn you!" flamed Kane suddenly, showing that his conscience had not been at rest. "Doubtless they will, being fools. Yet what could I do? Had I left it there, people might have starved and gone naked for lack of it. More, it would have been found, and theft and slaughter would have followed anyway. You are to blame, for had this treasure been left with its rightful owners, no such trouble would have ensued."

The Wolf grinned without reply. Kane not being a profane man, his rare curses had double effect and always startled his hearers, no matter how vicious or hardened they might be.

It was Kane who spoke next. "Why have you fled from me across the world? You do not really fear me."

"No, you are right. Really I do not know; perhaps flight is a habit which is difficult to break. I made my mistake when I did not kill you that night in the mountains. I am sure I could kill you in a fair fight, yet I have never even, ere now, sought to ambush you. Somehow I have not had a liking to meet you, Monsieur—a whim of mine, a mere whim. Then—*mon Dieu!*—mayhap I have enjoyed a new sensation—and I had thought that I had exhausted the thrills of life. And then, a man must either be the hunter or the hunted. Until now, Monsieur, I was the hunted, but I grew weary of the role—I thought I had thrown you off the trail."

"A negro slave, brought from this vicinity, told a Portugal ship captain of a white man who landed from a Spanish ship and went into the jungle. I heard of it and hired the ship, paying the captain to bring me here."

"Monsieur, I admire you for your attempt, but you must admire me, too! Alone I came into this village, and alone among savages and cannibals I—with some slight knowledge of the language learned from a

✝

slave aboard ship—I gained the confidence of King Songa and supplanted that mummer, N'Longa. I am a braver man than you, Monsieur, for I had no ship to retreat to, and a ship is waiting for you."

"I admire your courage," said Kane, "but you are content to rule amongst cannibals—you the blackest soul of them all. I intend to return to my own people when I have slain you."

"Your confidence would be admirable were it not amusing. Ho, Gulka!"

A giant negro stalked into the space between them. He was the hugest man that Kane had ever seen, though he moved with catlike ease and suppleness. His arms and legs were like trees, and the great, sinuous muscles rippled with each motion. His apelike head was set squarely between gigantic shoulders. His great, dusky hands were like the talons of an ape, and his brow slanted back from above bestial eyes. Flat nose and great, thick red lips completed this picture of primitive, lustful savagery.

"That is Gulka, the gorilla-slayer," said Le Loup. "He it was who lay in wait beside the trail and smote you down. You are like a wolf, yourself, Monsieur Kane, but since your ship hove in sight you have been watched by many eyes, and had you had all the powers of a leopard, you had not seen Gulka nor heard him. He hunts the most terrible and crafty of all beasts, in their native forests, far to the north, the beasts-who-walk-like-men—as that one, whom he slew some days since."

✝

Kane, following Le Loup's fingers, made out a curious, manlike thing, dangling from a roof-pole of a hut. A jagged end thrust through the thing's body held it there. Kane could scarcely distinguish its characteristics by the firelight, but there was a weird, humanlike semblance about the hideous, hairy thing.

"A female gorilla that Gulka slew and brought to the village," said Le Loup.

The giant black slouched close to Kane and stared into the white man's eyes. Kane returned his gaze somberly, and presently the negro's eyes dropped sullenly and he slouched back a few paces. The look in the Puritan's grim eyes had pierced the primitive hazes of the gorilla-slayer's soul, and for the first time in his life he felt fear. To throw this off, he tossed a challenging look about; then, with unexpected animalness, he struck his huge chest resoundingly, grinned cavernously and flexed his mighty arms. No one spoke. Primordial bestiality had the stage, and the more highly developed types looked on with various feelings of amusement, tolerance or contempt.

Gulka glanced furtively at Kane to see if the white man was watching him, then with a sudden beastly roar, plunged forward and dragged a man from the semicircle. While the trembling victim screeched for mercy, the giant hurled him upon the crude altar before the shadowy idol. A spear rose and flashed, and the screeching ceased.

The Black God looked on, his monstrous features seeming to leer in the flickering firelight. He had drunk; was the Black God pleased with the draft—with the sacrifice?

Gulka stalked back, and stopping before Kane, flourished the bloody spear before the white man's face.

Le Loup laughed. Then suddenly N'Longa appeared. He came from nowhere in particular; suddenly he was standing there, beside the post to which Kane was bound. A lifetime of study of the art of illusion had given the juju man a highly technical knowledge of appearing and disappearing—which after all, consisted only in timing the audience's attention.

He waved Gulka aside with a grand gesture, and the gorilla-man slunk back, apparently to get out of N'Longa's gaze—then with incredible swiftness he turned and struck the juju man a terrific blow upon the side of the head with his open hand. N'Longa went down like a felled ox, and in an instant he had been seized and bound to a post close to Kane. An uncertain murmuring rose from the negroes, which died out as King Songa stared angrily toward them.

Le Loup leaned back upon his throne and laughed uproariously.

"The trail ends here, Monsieur Galahad. That ancient fool thought I did not know of his plotting! I was hiding outside the hut and heard the

✝

interesting conversation you two had. Ha! ha! ha! ha! The Black God must drink, Monsieur, but I have persuaded Songa to have you two burnt; that will be much more enjoyable, though we shall have to forego the usual feast, I fear. For after the fires are lit about your feet the devil himself could not keep your carcasses from becoming charred frames of bone."

Songa shouted something imperiously, and blacks came bearing wood, which they piled about the feet of N'Longa and Kane. The juju man had recovered consciousness, and he now shouted something in his native language. Again the murmuring arose among the shadowy throng. Songa snarled something in reply.

Kane gazed at the scene almost impersonally. Again, somewhere in his soul, dim primal deeps were stirring, age-old thought memories, veiled in the fogs of lost eons. He had been here before, thought Kane; he knew all this of old—the lurid flames beating back the sullen night, the bestial faces leering expectantly, and the god, the Black God, there in the shadows! Always the Black God, brooding back in the shadows. He had known the shouts, the frenzied chant of the worshipers, back there in the gray dawn of the world, the speech of the bellowing drums, the singing priests, the repellent, inflaming, all-pervading scent of freshly

✝

spilt blood. All this have I known, somewhere, sometime, thought Kane; now I am the main actor—

He became aware that someone was speaking to him through the roar of the drums; he had not realized that the drums had begun to boom again. The speaker was N'Longa:

"Me pow'rful juju man! Watch now: I work mighty magic. Songa!" His voice rose in a screech that drowned out the wildly clamoring drums.

Songa grinned at the words N'Longa screamed at him. The chant of the drums now had dropped to a low, sinister monotone and Kane plainly heard Le Loup when he spoke:

"N'Longa says that he will now work that magic which it is death to speak, even. Never before has it been worked in the sight of living men; it is the nameless juju magic. Watch closely, Monsieur; possibly we shall be further amused." The Wolf laughed lightly and sardonically.

A black man stooped, applying a torch to the wood about Kane's feet. Tiny jets of flame began to leap up and catch. Another bent to do the same with N'Longa, then hesitated. The juju man sagged in his bonds; his head drooped upon his chest. He seemed dying.

Le Loup leaned forward, cursing, "Feet of the Devil! is the scoundrel about to cheat us of our pleasure of seeing him writhe in the flames?"

$\dagger$

The warrior gingerly touched the wizard and said something in his own language.

Le Loup laughed: "He died of fright. A great wizard, by the—"

His voice trailed off suddenly. The drums stopped as if the drummers had fallen dead simultaneously. Silence dropped like a fog upon the village and in the stillness Kane heard only the sharp crackle of the flames whose heat he was beginning to feel.

All eyes were turned upon the dead man upon the altar, *for the corpse had begun to move!*

First a twitching of a hand, then an aimless motion of an arm, a motion which gradually spread over the body and limbs. Slowly, with blind, uncertain gestures, the dead man turned upon his side, the trailing limbs found the earth. Then, horribly like something being born, like some frightful reptilian thing bursting the shell of nonexistence, the corpse tottered and reared upright, standing on legs wide apart and stiffly braced, arms still making useless, infantile motions. Utter silence, save somewhere a man's quick breath sounded loud in the stillness.

Kane stared, for the first time in his life smitten speechless and thoughtless. To his Puritan mind this was Satan's hand manifested.

Le Loup sat on his throne, eyes wide and staring, hand still half raised in the careless gesture he was making when frozen into silence by the unbelievable sight. Songa sat beside him, mouth and eyes wide open, fingers making curious jerky motions upon the carved arms of the throne.

Now the corpse was upright, swaying on stiltlike legs, body tilting far back until the sightless eyes seemed to stare straight into the red moon that was just rising over the black jungle. The thing tottered uncertainly in a wide, erratic half-circle, arms flung out grotesquely as if in balance, then swaying about to face the two thrones—and the Black God. A burning twig at Kane's feet cracked like the crash of a cannon in the tense silence. The horror thrust forth a black foot—it took a wavering step—another. Then with stiff, jerky and automatonlike steps, legs straddled far apart, the dead man came toward the two who sat in speechless horror to each side of the Black God.

"Ah-h-h!" from somewhere came the explosive sigh, from that shadowy semicircle where crouched the terror-fascinated worshippers. Straight on stalked the grim specter. Now it was within three strides of the thrones, and Le Loup, faced by fear for the first time in his bloody life, cringed back in his chair; while Songa, with a superhuman effort breaking the chains of horror that held him helpless, shattered the night with a wild scream and, springing to his feet, lifted a spear, shrieking and gibbering in wild menace. Then as the ghastly thing halted not its frightful advance, he hurled the spear with all the power of his great,

†

black muscles, and the spear tore through the dead man's breast with a rending of flesh and bone. Not an instant halted the thing—for the dead die not—and Songa the king stood frozen, arms outstretched as if to fend off the terror.

An instant they stood so, leaping firelight and eerie moonlight etching the scene forever in the minds of the beholders. The changeless staring eyes of the corpse looked full into the bulging eyes of Songa, where were reflected all the hells of horror. Then with a jerky motion the arms of the thing went out and up. The dead hands fell on Songa's shoulders. At the first touch, the king seemed to shrink and shrivel, and with a scream that was to haunt the dreams of every watcher through all the rest of time, Songa crumpled and fell, and the dead man reeled stiffly and fell with him. Motionless lay the two at the feet of the Black God, and to Kane's dazed mind it seemed that the idol's great, inhuman eyes were fixed upon them with terrible, still laughter.

At the instant of the king's fall, a great shout went up from the blacks, and Kane, with a clarity lent his subconscious mind by the depths of his hate, looked for Le Loup and saw him spring from his throne and vanish in the darkness. Then vision was blurred by a rush of black figures who swept into the space before the god. Feet knocked aside the blazing brands whose heat Kane had forgotten, and dusky hands freed him; others loosed the wizard's body and laid it upon the earth.

†

Kane dimly understood that the blacks believed this thing to be the work of N'Longa, and that they connected the vengeance of the wizard with himself. He bent, laid a hand on the juju man's shoulder. No doubt of it: he was dead, the flesh was already cold. He glanced at the other corpses. Songa was dead, too, and the thing that had slain him lay now without movement.

Kane started to rise, then halted. Was he dreaming, or did he really feel a sudden warmth in the dead flesh he touched? Mind reeling, he again bent over the wizard's body, and slowly he felt warmness steal over the limbs and the blood begin to flow sluggishly through the veins again.

Then N'Longa opened his eyes and stared up into Kane's, with the blank expression of a newborn babe. Kane watched, flesh crawling, and saw the knowing, reptilian glitter come back, saw the wizard's thick lips part in a wide grin. N'Longa sat up, and a strange chant arose from the negroes.

Kane looked about. The blacks were all kneeling, swaying their bodies to and fro, and in their shouts Kane caught the word, "N'Longa!" repeated over and over in a kind of fearsomely ecstatic refrain of terror and worship. As the wizard rose, they all fell prostrate.

N'Longa nodded, as if in satisfaction.

"Great juju—great fetish, me!" he announced to Kane. "You see? My ghost go out—kill Songa—come back to me! Great magic! Great fetish, me!"

Kane glanced at the Black God looming back in the shadows, at N'Longa, who now flung out his arms toward the idol as if in invocation.

I am everlasting (Kane thought the Black God said); I drink, no matter who rules; chiefs, slayers, wizards, they pass like the ghosts of dead men through the gray jungle; I stand, I rule; I am the soul of the jungle (said the Black God).

Suddenly Kane came back from the illusory mists in which he had been wandering. "The white man! Which way did he flee?"

N'Longa shouted something. A score of dusky hands pointed; from somewhere Kane's rapier was thrust out to him. The fogs faded and vanished; again he was the avenger, the scourge of the unrighteous; with the sudden volcanic speed of a tiger he snatched the sword and was gone.

$$\dagger$$

$$V$$

The End of the Red Trail

Limbs and vines slapped against Kane's face. The oppressive steam of the tropic night rose like mist about him. The moon, now floating high above the jungle, limned the black shadows in its white glow and patterned the jungle floor in grotesque designs. Kane knew not if the man he sought was ahead of him, but broken limbs and trampled underbrush showed that some man had gone that way, some man who fled in haste, nor halted to pick his way. Kane followed these signs unswervingly. Believing in the justice of his vengeance, he did not doubt that the dim beings who rule men's destinies would finally bring him face to face with Le Loup.

Behind him the drums boomed and muttered. What a tale they had to tell this night! of the triumph of N'Longa, the death of the black king, the overthrow of the white-man-with-eyes-like-a-leopard, and a more darksome tale, a tale to be whispered in low, muttering vibrations: the nameless juju.

Was he dreaming? Kane wondered as he hurried on. Was all this part of some foul magic? He had seen a dead man rise and slay and die again; he had seen a man die and come to life again. Did N'Longa in truth send

✝

his ghost, his soul, his life essence forth into the void, dominating a corpse to do his will? Aye, N'Longa died a real death there, bound to the torture stake, and he who lay dead on the altar rose and did as N'Longa would have done had he been free. Then, the unseen force animating the dead man fading, N'Longa had lived again.

Yes, Kane thought, he must admit it as a fact. Somewhere in the darksome reaches of jungle and river, N'Longa had stumbled upon the Secret—the Secret of controlling life and death, of overcoming the shackles and limitations of the flesh. How had this dark wisdom, born in the black and bloodstained shadows of this grim land, been given to the wizard? What sacrifice had been so pleasing to the Black Gods, what ritual so monstrous, as to make them give up the knowledge of this magic? And what thoughtless, timeless journeys had N'Longa taken, when he chose to send his ego, his ghost, through the far, misty countries, reached only by death?

There is wisdom in the shadows (brooded the drums), wisdom and magic; go into the darkness for wisdom; ancient magic shuns the light; we remember the lost ages (whispered the drums), ere man became wise and foolish; we remember the beast gods—the serpent gods and the ape gods and the nameless, the Black Gods, they who drank blood and whose voices roared through the shadowy hills, who feasted and lusted.

$$\dagger$$

The secrets of life and of death are theirs; we remember, we remember (sang the drums).

Kane heard them as he hastened on. The tale they told to the feathered black warriors farther up the river, he could not translate; but they spoke to him in their own way, and that language was deeper, more basic.

The moon, high in the dark blue skies, lighted his way and gave him a clear vision as he came out at last into a glade and saw Le Loup standing there. The Wolf's naked blade was a long gleam of silver in the moon, and he stood with shoulders thrown back, the old, defiant smile still on his face.

"A long trail, Monsieur," said he. "It began in the mountains of France; it ends in an African jungle. I have wearied of the game at last, Monsieur—and you die. I had not fled from the village, even, save that—I admit it freely—that damnable witchcraft of N'Longa's shook my nerves. More, I saw that the whole tribe would turn against me."

Kane advanced warily, wondering what dim, forgotten tinge of chivalry in the bandit's soul had caused him thus to take his chance in the open. He half suspected treachery, but his keen eyes could detect no shadow of movement in the jungle on either side of the glade.

†

"Monsieur, on guard!" Le Loup's voice was crisp. "Time that we ended this fool's dance about the world. Here we are alone."

The men were now within reach of each other, and Le Loup, in the midst of his sentence, suddenly plunged forward with the speed of light, thrusting viciously. A slower man had died there, but Kane parried and sent his own blade in a silver streak that slit Le Loup's tunic as the Wolf bounded backward. Le Loup admitted the failure of his trick with a wild laugh and came in with the breathtaking speed and fury of a tiger, his blade making a white fan of steel about him.

Rapier clashed on rapier as the two swordsmen fought. They were fire and ice opposed. Le Loup fought wildly but craftily, leaving no openings, taking advantage of every opportunity. He was a living flame, bounding back, leaping in, feinting, thrusting, warding, striking— laughing like a wild man, taunting and cursing.

Kane's skill was cold, calculating, scintillant. He made no waste movement, no motion not absolutely necessary. He seemed to devote more time and effort toward defense than did Le Loup, yet there was no hesitancy in his attack, and when he thrust, his blade shot out with the speed of a striking snake.

†

There was little to choose between the men as to height, strength and reach. Le Loup was the swifter by a scant, flashing margin, but Kane's skill reached a finer point of perfection. The Wolf's fencing was fiery, dynamic, like the blast from a furnace. Kane was more steady—less the instinctive, more the thinking fighter, though he, too, was a born slayer, with the coordination that only a natural fighter possessed.

Thrust, parry, a feint, a sudden whirl of blades—

"Ha!" the Wolf sent up a shout of ferocious laughter as the blood started from a cut on Kane's cheek. As if the sight drove him to further fury, he attacked like the beast men named him. Kane was forced back before that bloodlusting onslaught, but the Puritan's expression did not alter.

Minutes flew by; the clang and clash of steel did not diminish. Now they stood squarely in the center of the glade, Le Loup untouched, Kane's garments red with the blood that oozed from wounds on cheek, breast, arm and thigh. The Wolf grinned savagely and mockingly in the moonlight, but he had begun to doubt.

His breath came hissing fast and his arm began to weary; who was this man of steel and ice who never seemed to weaken? Le Loup knew that the wounds he had inflicted on Kane were not deep, but even so, the steady flow of blood should have sapped some of the man's strength and speed by this time. But if Kane felt the ebb of his powers, it did not

✝

show. His brooding countenance did not change in expression, and he pressed the fight with as much cold fury as at the beginning.

Le Loup felt his might fading, and with one last desperate effort he rallied all his fury and strength into a single plunge. A sudden, unexpected attack too wild and swift for the eye to follow, a dynamic burst of speed and fury no man could have withstood, and Solomon Kane reeled for the first time as he felt cold steel tear through his body. He reeled back, and Le Loup, with a wild shout, plunged after him, his reddened sword free, a gasping taunt on his lips.

Kane's sword, backed by the force of desperation, met Le Loup's in midair; met, held and wrenched. The Wolf's yell of triumph died on his lips as his sword flew singing from his hand.

For a fleeting instant he stopped short, arms flung wide as a crucifix, and Kane heard his wild, mocking laughter peal forth for the last time, as the Englishman's rapier made a silver line in the moonlight.

Far away came the mutter of the drums. Kane mechanically cleansed his sword on his tattered garments. The trail ended here, and Kane was conscious of a strange feeling of futility. He always felt that, after he had killed a foe. Somehow it always seemed that no real good had been wrought; as if the foe had, after all, escaped his just vengeance.

†

With a shrug of his shoulders Kane turned his attention to his bodily needs. Now that the heat of battle had passed, he began to feel weak and faint from the loss of blood. That last thrust had been close; had he not managed to avoid its full point by a twist of his body, the blade had transfixed him. As it was, the sword had struck glancingly, plowed along his ribs and sunk deep in the muscles beneath the shoulder-blade, inflicting a long, shallow wound.

Kane looked about him and saw that a small stream trickled through the glade at the far side. Here he made the only mistake of that kind that he ever made in his entire life. Mayhap he was dizzy from loss of blood and still mazed from the weird happenings of the night; be that as it may, he laid down his rapier and crossed, weaponless, to the stream. There he laved his wounds and bandaged them as best he could, with strips torn from his clothing.

Then he rose and was about to retrace his steps when a motion among the trees on the side of the glade where he first entered, caught his eye. A huge figure stepped out of the jungle, and Kane saw, and recognized, his doom. The man was Gulka, the gorilla-slayer. Kane remembered that he had not seen the black among those doing homage to N'Longa. How could he know the craft and hatred in that dusky, slanting skull that had led the negro, escaping the vengeance of his tribesmen, to trail down the only man he had ever feared? The Black God had been kind to his

46

neophyte; had led him upon his victim helpless and unarmed. Now Gulka could kill his man openly—and slowly, as a leopard kills, not smiting him down from ambush as he had planned, silently and suddenly.

A wide grin split the negro's face, and he moistened his lips. Kane, watching him, was coldly and deliberately weighing his chances. Gulka had already spied the rapiers. He was closer to them than was Kane. The Englishman knew that there was no chance of his winning in a sudden race for the swords.

A slow, deadly rage surged in him—the fury of helplessness. The blood churned in his temples and his eyes smoldered with a terrible light as he eyed the negro. His fingers spread and closed like claws. They were strong, those hands; men had died in their clutch. Even Gulka's huge black column of a neck might break like a rotten branch between them—a wave of weakness made the futility of these thoughts apparent to an extent that needed not the verification of the moonlight glimmering from the spear in Gulka's black hand. Kane could not even have fled had he wished—and he had never fled from a single foe.

The gorilla-slayer moved out into the glade. Massive, terrible, he was the personification of the primitive, the Stone Age. His mouth yawned in a red cavern of a grin; he bore himself with the haughty arrogance of savage might.

†

Kane tensed himself for the struggle that could end but one way. He strove to rally his waning forces. Useless; he had lost too much blood. At least he would meet his death on his feet, and somehow he stiffened his buckling knees and held himself erect, though the glade shimmered before him in uncertain waves and the moonlight seemed to have become a red fog through which he dimly glimpsed the approaching black man.

Kane stooped, though the effort nearly pitched him on his face; he dipped water in his cupped hands and dashed it into his face. This revived him, and he straightened, hoping that Gulka would charge and get it over with before his weakness crumpled him to the earth.

Gulka was now about the center of the glade, moving with the slow, easy stride of a great cat stalking a victim. He was not at all in a hurry to consummate his purpose. He wanted to toy with his victim, to see fear come into those grim eyes which had looked him down, even when the possessor of those eyes had been bound to the death stake. He wanted to slay, at last, slowly, glutting his tigerish bloodlust and torture-lust to the fullest extent.

Then suddenly he halted, turned swiftly, facing another side of the glade. Kane, wondering, followed his glance.

†

At first it seemed like a blacker shadow among the jungle shadows. At first there was no motion, no sound, but Kane instinctively knew that some terrible menace lurked there in the darkness that masked and merged the silent trees. A sullen horror brooded there, and Kane felt as if, from that monstrous shadow, inhuman eyes seared his very soul. Yet simultaneously there came the fantastic sensation that these eyes were not directed on him. He looked at the gorilla-slayer.

The black man had apparently forgotten him; he stood, half crouching, spear lifted, eyes fixed upon that clump of blackness. Kane looked again. Now there was motion in the shadows; they merged fantastically and moved out into the glade, much as Gulka had done. Kane blinked: was this the illusion that precedes death? The shape he looked upon was such as he had visioned dimly in wild nightmares, when the wings of sleep bore him back through lost ages.

He thought at first it was some blasphemous mockery of a man, for it went erect and was tall as a tall man. But it was inhumanly broad and thick, and its gigantic arms hung nearly to its misshapen feet. Then the moonlight smote full upon its bestial face, and Kane's mazed mind thought that the thing was the Black God coming out of the shadows, animated and bloodlusting. Then he saw that it was covered with hair, and he remembered the manlike thing dangling from the roof-pole in the native village. He looked at Gulka.

✝

The negro was facing the gorilla, spear at the charge. He was not afraid, but his sluggish mind was wondering over the miracle that brought this beast so far from his native jungles.

The mighty ape came out into the moonlight and there was a terrible majesty about his movements. He was nearer Kane than Gulka but he did not seem to be aware of the white man. His small, blazing eyes were fixed on the black man with terrible intensity. He advanced with a curious swaying stride.

Far away the drums whispered through the night, like an accompaniment to this grim Stone Age drama. The savage crouched in the middle of the glade, but the primordial came out of the jungle with eyes bloodshot and bloodlusting. The negro was face to face with a thing more primitive than he. Again ghosts of memories whispered to Kane: you have seen such sights before (they murmured), back in the dim days, the dawn days, when beast and beast-man battled for supremacy.

Gulka moved away from the ape in a half-circle, crouching, spear ready. With all his craft he was seeking to trick the gorilla, to make a swift kill, for he had never before met such a monster as this, and though he did not fear, he had begun to doubt. The ape made no attempt to stalk or circle; he strode straight forward toward Gulka.

✝

The black man who faced him and the white man who watched could not know the brutish love, the brutish hate that had driven the monster down from the low, forest-covered hills of the north to follow for leagues the trail of him who was the scourge of his kind—the slayer of his mate, whose body now hung from the roof-pole of the negro village.

The end came swiftly, almost like a sudden gesture. They were close, now, beast and beast-man; and suddenly, with an earthshaking roar, the gorilla charged. A great hairy arm smote aside the thrusting spear, and the ape closed with the negro. There was a shattering sound as of many branches breaking simultaneously, and Gulka slumped silently to the earth, to lie with arms, legs and body flung in strange, unnatural positions. The ape towered an instant above him, like a statue of the primordial triumphant.

Far away Kane heard the drums murmur. The soul of the jungle, the soul of the jungle: this phrase surged through his mind with monotonous reiteration.

The three who had stood in power before the Black God that night, where were they? Back in the village where the drums rustled lay Songa—King Songa, once lord of life and death, now a shriveled corpse with a face set in a mask of horror. Stretched on his back in the middle of the glade lay he whom Kane had followed many a league by land and sea. And Gulka the gorilla-slayer lay at the feet of his killer, broken at last by the savagery which had made him a true son of this grim land which had at last overwhelmed him.

Yet the Black God still reigned, thought Kane dizzily, brooding back in the shadows of this dark country, bestial, bloodlusting, caring naught who lived or died, so that he drank.

Kane watched the mighty ape, wondering how long it would be before the huge simian spied and charged him. But the gorilla gave no evidence of having even seen him. Some dim impulse of vengeance yet unglutted prompting him, he bent and raised the negro. Then he slouched toward the jungle, Gulka's limbs trailing limply and grotesquely. As he reached the trees, the ape halted, whirling the giant form high in the air with seemingly no effort, and dashed the dead man up among the branches. There was a rending sound as a broken projecting limb tore through the body hurled so powerfully against it, and the dead gorilla-slayer dangled there hideously.

A moment the clear moon limned the great ape in its glimmer, as he stood silently gazing up at his victim; then like a dark shadow he melted noiselessly into the jungle.

Kane walked slowly to the middle of the glade and took up his rapier. The blood had ceased to flow from his wounds, and some of his strength was returning, enough, at least, for him to reach the coast where his ship awaited him. He halted at the edge of the glade for a backward glance at Le Loup's upturned face and still form, white in the moonlight, and at the dark shadow among the trees that was Gulka, left by some bestial whim, hanging as the she-gorilla hung in the village.

Afar the drums muttered: "The wisdom of our land is ancient; the wisdom of our land is dark; whom we serve, we destroy. Flee if you would live, but you will never forget our chant. Never, never," sang the drums.

Kane turned to the trail which led to the beach and the ship waiting there.

†

Skulls in the Stars

I

He told how murderers walk the earth

Beneath the curse of Cain,

With crimson clouds before their eyes

And flames about their brain:

For blood has left upon their souls

Its everlasting stain.

Hood

There are two roads to Torkertown. One, the shorter and more direct route, leads across a barren upland moor, and the other, which is much longer, winds its tortuous way in and out among the hummocks and quagmires of the swamps, skirting the low hills to the east. It was a dangerous and tedious trail; so Solomon Kane halted in amazement when a breathless youth from the village he had just left, overtook him and implored him for God's sake to take the swamp road.

"The swamp road!" Kane stared at the boy.

✝

He was a tall, gaunt man, was Solomon Kane, his darkly pallid face and deep brooding eyes made more somber by the drab Puritanical garb he affected.

"Yes, sir, 'tis far safer," the youngster answered his surprised exclamation.

"Then the moor road must be haunted by Satan himself, for your townsmen warned me against traversing the other."

"Because of the quagmires, sir, that you might not see in the dark. You had better return to the village and continue your journey in the morning, sir."

"Taking the swamp road?"

"Yes, sir."

Kane shrugged his shoulders and shook his head.

"The moon rises almost as soon as twilight dies. By its light I can reach Torkertown in a few hours, across the moor."

"Sir, you had better not. No one ever goes that way. There are no houses at all upon the moor, while in the swamp there is the house of old Ezra who lives there all alone since his maniac cousin, Gideon, wandered off and died in the swamp and was never found—and old Ezra though a

†

miser would not refuse you lodging should you decide to stop until morning. Since you must go, you had better go the swamp road."

Kane eyed the boy piercingly. The lad squirmed and shuffled his feet.

"Since this moor road is so dour to wayfarers," said the Puritan, "why did not the villagers tell me the whole tale, instead of vague mouthings?"

"Men like not to talk of it, sir. We hoped that you would take the swamp road after the men advised you to, but when we watched and saw that you turned not at the forks, they sent me to run after you and beg you to reconsider."

"Name of the Devil!" exclaimed Kane sharply, the unaccustomed oath showing his irritation; "the swamp road and the moor road—what is it that threatens me and why should I go miles out of my way and risk the bogs and mires?"

"Sir," said the boy, dropping his voice and drawing closer, "we be simple villagers who like not to talk of such things lest foul fortune befall us, but the moor road is a way accurst and hath not been traversed by any of the countryside for a year or more. It is death to walk those moors by night, as hath been found by some score of unfortunates. Some foul horror haunts the way and claims men for his victims."

"So? And what is this thing like?"

$\dagger$

"No man knows. None has ever seen it and lived, but late-farers have heard terrible laughter far out on the fen and men have heard the horrid shrieks of its victims. Sir, in God's name return to the village, there pass the night, and tomorrow take the swamp trail to Torkertown."

Far back in Kane's gloomy eyes a scintillant light had begun to glimmer, like a witch's torch glinting under fathoms of cold gray ice. His blood quickened. Adventure! The lure of life-risk and battle! The thrill of breathtaking, touch-and-go drama! Not that Kane recognized his sensations as such. He sincerely considered that he voiced his real feelings when he said:

"These things be deeds of some power of evil. The lords of darkness have laid a curse upon the country. A strong man is needed to combat Satan and his might. Therefore I go, who have defied him many a time."

"Sir," the boy began, then closed his mouth as he saw the futility of argument. He only added, "The corpses of the victims are bruised and torn, sir."

He stood there at the crossroads, sighing regretfully as he watched the tall, rangy figure swinging up the road that led toward the moors.

The sun was setting as Kane came over the brow of the low hill which debouched into the upland fen. Huge and bloodred it sank down behind the sullen horizon of the moors, seeming to touch the rank grass with fire; so for a moment the watcher seemed to be gazing out across a sea of blood. Then the dark shadows came gliding from the east, the western blaze faded, and Solomon Kane struck out boldly in the gathering darkness.

The road was dim from disuse but was clearly defined. Kane went swiftly but warily, sword and pistols at hand. Stars blinked out and night winds whispered among the grass like weeping specters. The moon began to rise, lean and haggard, like a skull among the stars.

Then suddenly Kane stopped short. From somewhere in front of him sounded a strange and eerie echo—or something like an echo. Again, this time louder. Kane started forward again. Were his senses deceiving him? No!

Far out, there pealed a whisper of frightful laughter. And again, closer this time. No human being ever laughed like that—there was no mirth in it, only hatred and horror and soul-destroying terror. Kane halted. He was not afraid, but for the second he was almost unnerved. Then, stabbing through that awesome laughter, came the sound of a scream that was undoubtedly human. Kane started forward, increasing his gait. He cursed the illusive lights and flickering shadows which veiled the moor in the rising moon and made accurate sight impossible.

†

The laughter continued, growing louder, as did the screams. Then sounded faintly the drum of frantic human feet. Kane broke into a run.

Some human was being hunted to his death out there on the fen, and by what manner of horror God alone knew. The sound of the flying feet halted abruptly and the screaming rose unbearably, mingled with other sounds unnamable and hideous. Evidently the man had been overtaken, and Kane, his flesh crawling, visualized some ghastly fiend of the darkness crouching on the back of its victim—crouching and tearing.

Then the noise of a terrible and short struggle came clearly through the abysmal silence of the fen and the footfalls began again, but stumbling and uneven. The screaming continued, but with a gasping gurgle. The sweat stood cold on Kane's forehead and body. This was heaping horror on horror in an intolerable manner.

God, for a moment's clear light! The frightful drama was being enacted within a very short distance of him, to judge by the ease with which the sounds reached him. But this hellish half-light veiled all in shifting shadows, so that the moors appeared a haze of blurred illusions, and stunted trees and bushes seemed like giants.

Kane shouted, striving to increase the speed of his advance. The shrieks of the unknown broke into a hideous shrill squealing; again there was the sound of a struggle, and then from the shadows of the tall grass a thing came reeling—a thing that had once been a man—a gore-covered,

†

frightful thing that fell at Kane's feet and writhed and groveled and raised its terrible face to the rising moon, and gibbered and yammered, and fell down again and died in its own blood.

The moon was up now and the light was better. Kane bent above the body, which lay stark in its unnamable mutilation, and he shuddered—a rare thing for him, who had seen the deeds of the Spanish Inquisition and the witch-finders.

Some wayfarer, he supposed. Then like a hand of ice on his spine he was aware that he was not alone. He looked up, his cold eyes piercing the shadows whence the dead man had staggered. He saw nothing, but he knew—he felt—that other eyes gave back his stare, terrible eyes not of this earth. He straightened and drew a pistol, waiting. The moonlight spread like a lake of pale blood over the moor, and trees and grasses took on their proper sizes.

The shadows melted, and Kane *saw*! At first he thought it only a shadow of mist, a wisp of moor fog that swayed in the tall grass before him. He gazed. More illusion, he thought. Then the thing began to take on shape, vague and indistinct. Two hideous eyes flamed at him—eyes which held all the stark horror which has been the heritage of man since the fearful dawn ages—eyes frightful and insane, with an insanity transcending earthly insanity. The form of the thing was misty and

†

vague, a brain-shattering travesty on the human form, like, yet horridly unlike. The grass and bushes beyond showed clearly through it.

Kane felt the blood pound in his temples, yet he was as cold as ice. How such an unstable being as that which wavered before him could harm a man in a physical way was more than he could understand, yet the red horror at his feet gave mute testimony that the fiend could act with terrible material effect.

Of one thing Kane was sure: there would be no hunting of him across the dreary moors, no screaming and fleeing to be dragged down again and again. If he must die he would die in his tracks, his wounds in front.

Now a vague and grisly mouth gaped wide and the demoniac laughter again shrieked out, soul-shaking in its nearness. And in the midst of that threat of doom, Kane deliberately leveled his long pistol and fired. A maniacal yell of rage and mockery answered the report, and the thing came at him like a flying sheet of smoke, long shadowy arms stretched to drag him down.

Kane, moving with the dynamic speed of a famished wolf, fired the second pistol with as little effect, snatched his long rapier from its sheath and thrust into the center of the misty attacker. The blade sang as it passed clear through, encountering no solid resistance, and Kane felt icy fingers grip his limbs, bestial talons tear his garments and the skin beneath.

†

He dropped the useless sword and sought to grapple with his foe. It was like fighting a floating mist, a flying shadow armed with daggerlike claws. His savage blows met empty air, his leanly mighty arms, in whose grasp strong men had died, swept nothingness and clutched emptiness. Naught was solid or real save the flaying, apelike fingers with their crooked talons, and the crazy eyes which burned into the shuddering depths of his soul.

Kane realized that he was in a desperate plight indeed. Already his garments hung in tatters and he bled from a score of deep wounds. But he never flinched, and the thought of flight never entered his mind. He had never fled from a single foe, and had the thought occurred to him he would have flushed with shame.

He saw no help for it now, but that his form should lie there beside the fragments of the other victim, but the thought held no terrors for him. His only wish was to give as good an account of himself as possible before the end came, and if he could, to inflict some damage on his unearthly foe.

There above the dead man's torn body, man fought with demon under the pale light of the rising moon, with all the advantages with the demon, save one. And that one was enough to overcome all the others. For if abstract hate may bring into material substance a ghostly thing,

✝

may not courage, equally abstract, form a concrete weapon to combat that ghost?

Kane fought with his arms and his feet and his hands, and he was aware at last that the ghost began to give back before him, that the fearful laughter changed to screams of baffled fury. For man's only weapon is courage that flinches not from the gates of Hell itself, and against such not even the legions of Hell can stand.

Of this Kane knew nothing; he only knew that the talons which tore and rended him seemed to grow weaker and wavering, that a wild light grew and grew in the horrible eyes. And reeling and gasping, he rushed in, grappled the thing at last and threw it, and as they tumbled about on the moor and it writhed and lapped his limbs like a serpent of smoke, his flesh crawled and his hair stood on end, for he began to understand its gibbering.

He did not hear and comprehend as a man hears and comprehends the speech of a man, but the frightful secrets it imparted in whisperings and yammerings and screaming silences sank fingers of ice and flame into his soul, and he *knew*.

†

II

The hut of old Ezra the miser stood by the road in the midst of the swamp, half screened by the sullen trees which grew about it. The walls were rotting, the roof crumbling, and great, pallid and green fungus-monsters clung to it and writhed about the doors and windows, as if seeking to peer within. The trees leaned above it and their gray branches intertwined so that it crouched in the semidarkness like a monstrous dwarf over whose shoulder ogres leer.

The road which wound down into the swamp, among rotting stumps and rank hummocks and scummy, snake-haunted pools and bogs, crawled past the hut. Many people passed that way these days, but few saw old Ezra, save a glimpse of a yellow face, peering through the fungus-screened windows, itself like an ugly fungus.

Old Ezra the miser partook much of the quality of the swamp, for he was gnarled and bent and sullen; his fingers were like clutching parasitic plants and his locks hung like drab moss above eyes trained to the murk of the swamplands. His eyes were like a dead man's, yet hinted of depths abysmal and loathsome as the dead lakes of the swamplands.

These eyes gleamed now at the man who stood in front of his hut. This man was tall and gaunt and dark, his face was haggard and claw-marked,

✝

and he was bandaged of arm and leg. Somewhat behind this man stood a number of villagers.

"You are Ezra of the swamp road?"

"Aye, and what want ye of me?"

"Where is your cousin Gideon, the maniac youth who abode with you?"

"Gideon?"

"Aye."

"He wandered away into the swamp and never came back. No doubt he lost his way and was set upon by wolves or died in a quagmire or was struck by an adder."

"How long ago?"

"Over a year."

"Aye. Hark ye, Ezra the miser. Soon after your cousin's disappearance, a countryman, coming home across the moors, was set upon by some unknown fiend and torn to pieces, and thereafter it became death to cross those moors. First men of the countryside, then strangers who wandered over the fen, fell to the clutches of the thing. Many men have died, since the first one.

$$\dagger$$

"Last night I crossed the moors, and heard the flight and pursuing of another victim, a stranger who knew not the evil of the moors. Ezra the miser, it was a fearful thing, for the wretch twice broke from the fiend, terribly wounded, and each time the demon caught and dragged him down again. And at last he fell dead at my very feet, done to death in a manner that would freeze the statue of a saint."

The villagers moved restlessly and murmured fearfully to each other, and old Ezra's eyes shifted furtively. Yet the somber expression of Solomon Kane never altered, and his condor-like stare seemed to transfix the miser.

"Aye, aye!" muttered old Ezra hurriedly; "a bad thing, a bad thing! Yet why do you tell this thing to me?"

"Aye, a sad thing. Harken further, Ezra. The fiend came out of the shadows and I fought with it, over the body of its victim. Aye, how I overcame it, I know not, for the battle was hard and long, but the powers of good and light were on my side, which are mightier than the powers of Hell.

"At the last I was stronger, and it broke from me and fled, and I followed to no avail. Yet before it fled it whispered to me a monstrous truth."

Old Ezra started, stared wildly, seemed to shrink into himself.

"Nay, why tell me this?" he muttered.

†

"I returned to the village and told my tale," said Kane, "for I knew that now I had the power to rid the moors of its curse forever. Ezra, come with us!"

"Where?" gasped the miser.

"*To the rotting oak on the moors.*"

Ezra reeled as though struck; he screamed incoherently and turned to flee.

On the instant, at Kane's sharp order, two brawny villagers sprang forward and seized the miser. They twisted the dagger from his withered hand, and pinioned his arms, shuddering as their fingers encountered his clammy flesh.

Kane motioned them to follow, and turning strode up the trail, followed by the villagers, who found their strength taxed to the utmost in their task of bearing their prisoner along. Through the swamp they went and out, taking a little-used trail which led up over the low hills and out on the moors.

The sun was sliding down the horizon and old Ezra stared at it with bulging eyes—stared as if he could not gaze enough. Far out on the moors reared up the great oak tree, like a gibbet, now only a decaying shell. There Solomon Kane halted.

✝

Old Ezra writhed in his captor's grasp and made inarticulate noises.

"Over a year ago," said Solomon Kane, "you, fearing that your insane cousin Gideon would tell men of your cruelties to him, brought him away from the swamp by the very trail by which we came, and murdered him here in the night."

Ezra cringed and snarled.

"You can not prove this lie!"

Kane spoke a few words to an agile villager. The youth clambered up the rotting bole of the tree and from a crevice, high up, dragged something that fell with a clatter at the feet of the miser. Ezra went limp with a terrible shriek.

The object was a man's skeleton, the skull cleft.

"You—how knew you this? You are Satan!" gibbered old Ezra.

Kane folded his arms.

"The thing I fought last night told me this thing as we reeled in battle, and I followed it to this tree. *For the fiend is Gideon's ghost.*"

Ezra shrieked again and fought savagely.

"You knew," said Kane somberly, "you knew what thing did these deeds. You feared the ghost of the maniac, and that is why you chose to leave his body on the fen instead of concealing it in the swamp.

✝

For you knew the ghost would haunt the place of his death. He was insane in life, and in death he did not know where to find his slayer; else he had come to you in your hut. He hates no man but you, but his mazed spirit can not tell one man from another, and he slays all, lest he let his killer escape. Yet he will know you and rest in peace forever after. Hate hath made of his ghost a solid thing that can rend and slay, and though he feared you terribly in life, in death he fears you not."

Kane halted. He glanced at the sun.

"All this I had from Gideon's ghost, in his yammerings and his whisperings and his shrieking silences. Naught but your death will lay that ghost."

Ezra listened in breathless silence and Kane pronounced the words of his doom.

"A hard thing it is," said Kane somberly, "to sentence a man to death in cold blood and in such a manner as I have in mind, but you must die that others may live—and God knoweth you deserve death.

"You shall not die by noose, bullet or sword, but at the talons of him you slew—for naught else will satiate him."

At these words Ezra's brain shattered, his knees gave way and he fell groveling and screaming for death, begging them to burn him at the stake, to flay him alive. Kane's face was set like death, and the villagers,

$\dagger$

the fear rousing their cruelty, bound the screeching wretch to the oak tree, and one of them bade him make his peace with God. But Ezra made no answer, shrieking in a high shrill voice with unbearable monotony. Then the villager would have struck the miser across the face, but Kane stayed him.

"Let him make his peace with Satan, whom he is more like to meet," said the Puritan grimly. "The sun is about to set. Loose his cords so that he may work loose by dark, since it is better to meet death free and unshackled than bound like a sacrifice."

As they turned to leave him, old Ezra yammered and gibbered unhuman sounds and then fell silent, staring at the sun with terrible intensity.

They walked away across the fen, and Kane flung a last look at the grotesque form bound to the tree, seeming in the uncertain light like a great fungus growing to the bole. And suddenly the miser screamed hideously:

"Death! Death! There are skulls in the stars!"

"Life was good to him, though he was gnarled and churlish and evil," Kane sighed. "Mayhap God has a place for such souls where fire and sacrifice may cleanse them of their dross as fire cleans the forest of fungous things. Yet my heart is heavy within me."

✝

"Nay, sir," one of the villagers spoke, "you have done but the will of God, and good alone shall come of this night's deed."

"Nay," answered Kane heavily, "I know not—I know not."

The sun had gone down and night spread with amazing swiftness, as if great shadows came rushing down from unknown voids to cloak the world with hurrying darkness. Through the thick night came a weird echo, and the men halted and looked back the way they had come.

Nothing could be seen. The moor was an ocean of shadows and the tall grass about them bent in long waves before the faint wind, breaking the deathly stillness with breathless murmurings.

Then far away the red disk of the moon rose over the fen, and for an instant a grim silhouette was etched blackly against it. A shape came flying across the face of the moon—a bent, grotesque thing whose feet seemed scarcely to touch the earth; and close behind came a thing like a flying shadow—a nameless, shapeless horror.

A moment the racing twain stood out boldly against the moon; then they merged into one unnamable, formless mass, and vanished in the shadows.

Far across the fen sounded a single shriek of terrible laughter.

✝

Rattle of Bones

"**L**andlord, ho!" The shout broke the lowering silence and reverberated through the black forest with sinister echoing.

"This place hath a forbidding aspect, meseemeth."

Two men stood in front of the forest tavern. The building was low, long and rambling, built of heavy logs. Its small windows were heavily barred and the door was closed. Above the door its sinister sign showed faintly—a cleft skull.

This door swung slowly open and a bearded face peered out. The owner of the face stepped back and motioned his guests to enter—with a grudging gesture it seemed. A candle gleamed on a table; a flame smoldered in the fireplace.

"Your names?"

"Solomon Kane," said the taller man briefly.

"Gaston l'Armon," the other spoke curtly. "But what is that to you?"

"Strangers are few in the Black Forest," grunted the host, "bandits many. Sit at yonder table and I will bring food."

†

The two men sat down, with the bearing of men who have traveled far. One was a tall gaunt man, clad in a featherless hat and somber black garments, which set off the dark pallor of his forbidding face. The other was of a different type entirely, bedecked with lace and plumes, although his finery was somewhat stained from travel. He was handsome in a bold way, and his restless eyes shifted from side to side, never still an instant.

The host brought wine and food to the rough-hewn table and then stood back in the shadows, like a somber image. His features, now receding into vagueness, now luridly etched in the firelight as it leaped and flickered, were masked in a beard which seemed almost animal-like in thickness. A great nose curved above this beard and two small red eyes stared unblinkingly at his guests.

"Who are you?" suddenly asked the younger man.

"I am the host of the Cleft Skull Tavern," sullenly replied the other. His tone seemed to challenge his questioner to ask further.

"Do you have many guests?" l'Armon pursued.

"Few come twice," the host grunted.

Kane started and glanced up straight into those small red eyes, as if he sought for some hidden meaning in the host's words.

†

The flaming eyes seemed to dilate, then dropped sullenly before the Englishman's cold stare.

"I'm for bed," said Kane abruptly, bringing his meal to a close. "I must take up my journey by daylight."

"And I," added the Frenchman. "Host, show us to our chambers."

Black shadows wavered on the walls as the two followed their silent host down a long, dark hall. The stocky, broad body of their guide seemed to grow and expand in the light of the small candle which he carried, throwing a long, grim shadow behind him.

At a certain door he halted, indicating that they were to sleep there. They entered; the host lit a candle with the one he carried, then lurched back the way he had come.

In the chamber the two men glanced at each other. The only furnishings of the room were a couple of bunks, a chair or two and a heavy table.

"Let us see if there be any way to make fast the door," said Kane. "I like not the looks of mine host."

"There are racks on door and jamb for a bar," said Gaston, "but no bar."

✝

"We might break up the table and use its pieces for a bar," mused Kane.

"*Mon Dieu*," said l'Armon, "you are timorous, *m'sieu.*"

Kane scowled. "I like not being murdered in my sleep," he answered gruffly.

"My faith!" the Frenchman laughed. "We are chance met—until I overtook you on the forest road an hour before sunset, we had never seen each other."

"I have seen you somewhere before," answered Kane, "though I can not now recall where. As for the other, I assume every man is an honest fellow until he shows me he is a rogue; moreover, I am a light sleeper and slumber with a pistol at hand."

The Frenchman laughed again.

"I was wondering how *m'sieu* could bring himself to sleep in the room with a stranger! Ha! Ha! All right, *m'sieu* Englishman, let us go forth and take a bar from one of the other rooms."

Taking the candle with them, they went into the corridor. Utter silence reigned and the small candle twinkled redly and evilly in the thick darkness.

✝

"Mine host hath neither guests nor servants," muttered Solomon Kane. "A strange tavern! What is the name, now? These German words come not easily to me—the Cleft Skull? A bloody name, i'faith."

They tried the rooms next to theirs, but no bar rewarded their search. At last they came to the last room at the end of the corridor. They entered. It was furnished like the rest, except that the door was provided with a small barred opening, and fastened from the outside with a heavy bolt, which was secured at one end to the doorjamb. They raised the bolt and looked in.

"There should be an outer window, but there is not," muttered Kane. "Look!"

The floor was stained darkly. The walls and the one bunk were hacked in places, great splinters having been torn away.

"Men have died in here," said Kane, somberly. "Is yonder not a bar fixed in the wall?"

"Aye, but 'tis made fast," said the Frenchman, tugging at it. "The—"

A section of the wall swung back and Gaston gave a quick exclamation. A small, secret room was revealed, and the two men bent over the grisly thing that lay upon its floor.

"The skeleton of a man!" said Gaston. "And behold, how his bony leg is shackled to the floor! He was imprisoned here and died."

✝

"Nay," said Kane, "the skull is cleft—methinks mine host had a grim reason for the name of his hellish tavern. This man, like us, was no doubt a wanderer who fell into the fiend's hands."

"Likely," said Gaston without interest; he was engaged in idly working the great iron ring from the skeleton's leg bones. Failing in this, he drew his sword and with an exhibition of remarkable strength cut the chain which joined the ring on the leg to a ring set deep in the log floor.

"Why should he shackle a skeleton to the floor?" mused the Frenchman. "*Monbleu!* 'Tis a waste of good chain. Now, *m'sieu*," he ironically addressed the white heap of bones, "I have freed you and you may go where you like!"

"Have done!" Kane's voice was deep. "No good will come of mocking the dead."

"The dead should defend themselves," laughed l'Armon. "Somehow, I will slay the man who kills me, though my corpse climb up forty fathoms of ocean to do it."

Kane turned toward the outer door, closing the door of the secret room behind him. He liked not this talk which smacked of demonry and witchcraft; and he was in haste to face the host with the charge of his guilt.

✝

As he turned, with his back to the Frenchman, he felt the touch of cold steel against his neck and knew that a pistol muzzle was pressed close beneath the base of his brain.

"Move not, *m'sieu*!" The voice was low and silky. "Move not, or I will scatter your few brains over the room."

The Puritan, raging inwardly, stood with his hands in air while l'Armon slipped his pistols and sword from their sheaths.

"Now you can turn," said Gaston, stepping back.

Kane bent a grim eye on the dapper fellow, who stood bareheaded now, hat in one hand, the other hand leveling his long pistol.

"Gaston the Butcher!" said the Englishman somberly. "Fool that I was to trust a Frenchman! You range far, murderer! I remember you now, with that cursed great hat off—I saw you in Calais some years agone."

"Aye—and now you will see me never again. What was that?"

"Rats exploring yon skeleton," said Kane, watching the bandit like a hawk, waiting for a single slight wavering of that black gun muzzle. "The sound was of the rattle of bones."

"Like enough," returned the other. "Now, M'sieu Kane, I know you carry considerable money on your person. I had thought to wait until you slept and then slay you, but the opportunity presented itself and I took it. You trick easily."

"I had little thought that I should fear a man with whom I had broken bread," said Kane, a deep timbre of slow fury sounding in his voice.

The bandit laughed cynically. His eyes narrowed as he began to back slowly toward the outer door. Kane's sinews tensed involuntarily; he gathered himself like a giant wolf about to launch himself in a death leap, but Gaston's hand was like a rock and the pistol never trembled.

"We will have no death plunges after the shot," said Gaston. "Stand still, *m'sieu*, I have seen men killed by dying men, and I wish to have distance enough between us to preclude that possibility. My faith—I will shoot, you will roar and charge, but you will die before you reach me with your bare hands. And mine host will have another skeleton in his secret niche. That is, if I do not kill him myself. The fool knows me not nor I him, moreover—"

The Frenchman was in the doorway now, sighting along the barrel. The candle, which had been stuck in a niche on the wall, shed a weird and flickering light which did not extend past the doorway. And with the suddenness of death, from the darkness behind Gaston's back, a broad, vague form rose up and a gleaming blade swept down. The Frenchman went to his knees like a butchered ox, his brains spilling from his cleft

†

skull. Above him towered the figure of the host, a wild and terrible spectacle, still holding the hanger with which he had slain the bandit.

"Ho! ho!" he roared. "Back!"

Kane had leaped forward as Gaston fell, but the host thrust into his very face a long pistol which he held in his left hand.

"Back!" he repeated in a tigerish roar, and Kane retreated from the menacing weapon and the insanity in the red eyes.

The Englishman stood silent, his flesh crawling as he sensed a deeper and more hideous threat than the Frenchman had offered. There was something inhuman about this man, who now swayed to and fro like some great forest beast while his mirthless laughter boomed out again.

"Gaston the Butcher!" he shouted, kicking the corpse at his feet. "Ho! ho! My fine brigand will hunt no more! I had heard of this fool who roamed the Black Forest—he wished gold and he found death! Now your gold shall be mine; and more than gold—vengeance!"

"I am no foe of yours," Kane spoke calmly.

"All men are my foes! Look—the marks on my wrists! See—the marks on my ankles! And deep in my back—the kiss of the knout! And deep in my brain, the wounds of the years of the cold, silent cells where I lay as punishment for a crime I never committed!" The voice broke in a hideous, grotesque sob.

†

Kane made no answer. This man was not the first he had seen whose brain had shattered amid the horrors of the terrible Continental prisons.

"But I escaped!" the scream rose triumphantly, "and here I make war on all men…. What was that?"

Did Kane see a flash of fear in those hideous eyes?

"My sorcerer is rattling his bones!" whispered the host, then laughed wildly. "Dying, he swore his very bones would weave a net of death for me. I shackled his corpse to the floor, and now, deep in the night, I hear his bare skeleton clash and rattle as he seeks to be free, and I laugh, I laugh! Ho! ho! How he yearns to rise and stalk like old King Death along these dark corridors when I sleep, to slay me in my bed!"

Suddenly the insane eyes flared hideously: "You were in that secret room, you and this dead fool! Did he talk to you?"

Kane shuddered in spite of himself. Was it insanity or did he actually hear the faint rattle of bones, as if the skeleton had moved slightly? Kane shrugged his shoulders; rats will even tug at dusty bones.

The host was laughing again. He sidled around Kane, keeping the Englishman always covered, and with his free hand opened the door. All was darkness within, so that Kane could not even see the glimmer of the bones on the floor.

✝

"All men are my foes!" mumbled the host, in the incoherent manner of the insane. "Why should I spare any man? Who lifted a hand to my aid when I lay for years in the vile dungeons of Karlsruhe—and for a deed never proven? Something happened to my brain, then. I became as a wolf—a brother to these of the Black Forest to which I fled when I escaped.

"They have feasted, my brothers, on all who lay in my tavern—all except this one who now clashes his bones, this magician from Russia. Lest he come stalking back through the black shadows when night is over the world, and slay me—for who may slay the dead?—I stripped his bones and shackled him. His sorcery was not powerful enough to save him from me, but all men know that a dead magician is more evil than a living one. Move not, Englishman! Your bones I shall leave in this secret room beside this one, to—"

The maniac was standing partly in the doorway of the secret room, now, his weapon still menacing Kane. Suddenly he seemed to topple backward, and vanished in the darkness; and at the same instant a vagrant gust of wind swept down the outer corridor and slammed the door shut behind him. The candle on the wall flickered and went out. Kane's groping hands, sweeping over the floor, found a pistol, and he straightened, facing the door where the maniac had vanished. He stood in the utter darkness, his blood freezing, while a hideous muffled

†

screaming came from the secret room, intermingled with the dry, grisly

rattle of fleshless bones. Then silence fell.

Kane found flint and steel and lighted the candle. Then, holding it in

one hand and the pistol in the other, he opened the secret door.

"Great God!" he muttered as cold sweat formed on his body. "This

thing is beyond all reason, yet with mine own eyes I see it! Two vows

have here been kept, for Gaston the Butcher swore that even in death he

would avenge his slaying, and his was the hand which set yon fleshless

monster free. And he—"

The host of the Cleft Skull lay lifeless on the floor of the secret room,

his bestial face set in lines of terrible fear; and deep in his broken neck

were sunk the bare fingerbones of the sorcerer's skeleton.